Disney

Tangled
The Series

Best
LOOK AND FIND
Ever

we make books come alive®

pi kids® **Phoenix International Publications, Inc.**

Chicago • London • New York • Hamburg • Mexico City • Paris • Sydney

Rapunzel knows there is more in her. She has worked hard to become talented in a lot of different ways, and she isn't finished learning! Take a look and find these tools and helpers that assist the princess as she pursues her passions:

tiara

pencil

book

bow and arrow

Queen Arianna

Maximus

paintbrush

frying pan

paints

Cassandra

Plus est en vous

There is more in you

THINK AND SHARE!

★ WHICH OF THESE IMAGES OF RAPUNZEL IS THE MOST LIKE YOU? WHICH IS THE LEAST? WHY? (GO AHEAD AND PICK MORE THAN ONE IF YOU WANT!)

★ WHAT ARE THE THINGS YOU'VE WORKED HARD TO ACHIEVE?

★ WHAT WOULD YOU LOVE TO BE ABLE TO DO?

Cassandra is no ordinary handmaiden. She is also a highly trained swordswoman with a taste for adventure! She and her best friend Rapunzel (or "Raps" for short) may have to play it regal in the palace, but they can't wait to get out and make their mark on the world! Search around the castle for Cassandra and these other folks:

Cassandra and Rapunzel

Pascal

King Frederic

Queen Arianna

Captain of the Guard

Eugene

Business by day,

ADVENTURE BY NIGHT

THINK AND SHARE!

DO YOU KNOW THESE FUN FACTS ABOUT RAPUNZEL'S BEST FRIEND?

1. WHAT IS THE NAME OF CASSANDRA'S HORSE?
2. CASSANDRA WAS ADOPTED AS A BABY. WHO ADOPTED HER?
3. CASSANDRA HAS AN ANIMAL HELPER WHO ACTS AS HER "EYES IN THE SKY." WHAT KIND OF ANIMAL IS IT?
4. WHAT IS CASSANDRA'S WARRIOR NAME WHEN SHE COMPETES IN THE CHALLENGE OF THE BRAVE?
5. WHAT IS THE NAME OF THE WIZARD CASSANDRA INTRODUCES RAPUNZEL TO?

FIDELLA, THE CAPTAIN OF THE GUARD, OWL, THE IRON HANDMAIDEN, VARIAN.

NOW THINK OF 5 TRIVIA QUESTIONS ABOUT **YOU**! ASK YOUR FRIENDS AND FAMILY. HOW MANY CAN THEY GET RIGHT?

Friends HAVE EACH OTHER'S BACKS

Pascal, Fidella, and Maximus are very special to Rapunzel, Cassandra, and Eugene! Each is one of a kind...but look closely and you might see double. Can you find two identical images of each animal pal?

THINK AND SHARE!

★ DO YOU HAVE ANY PETS?

★ IF YOU COULD HAVE ANY PET IN THE WORLD, WHAT WOULD IT BE? WHY?

★ WRITE IT! TRY WRITING A LETTER FROM PASCAL TO RAPUNZEL. WHAT WOULD HE WANT TO TELL HER IF HE COULD TALK?

Rapunzel's long, golden hair magically returns, but does it trip her up? Not at all! She has been around the locks and knows how to use them to her advantage. Can you find these things curled up in her curls?

chalice

treasure box

teacup

paintbrush

mirror

frying pan

tiara

this flower

apple

pencil

YOU *can do* ANYTHING
YOU *put your hair to*

THINK AND SHARE!

★ WOULD YOU LIKE TO HAVE HAIR LIKE RAPUNZEL'S?

★ WHAT WOULD BE GREAT ABOUT IT?

★ WHAT WOULD BE NOT SO GREAT?

★ WRITE IT! WRITE A POEM ABOUT WHAT IT WOULD BE LIKE TO HAVE RAPUNZEL'S HAIR.

★ TRY IT! STYLE YOUR HAIR IN A WAY THAT'S UNIQUELY **YOU**. TAKE A PHOTO OF HOW YOU LOOK!

Rapunzel and her mother Queen Arianna have a lot in common! The Queen wishes a life filled with adventure for Rapunzel because that's what Rapunzel wishes for herself! Can you find these royal items?

goblet

tiara

hourglass

bugle

mirror

purse

this lantern

banner

Take on the WORLD

THINK AND SHARE!

★ WHO IS YOUR ROLE MODEL?

★ IN WHAT WAYS ARE YOU AND YOUR ROLE MODEL ALIKE?

★ HOW ARE YOU AND YOUR ROLE MODEL DIFFERENT?

★ WHAT QUESTIONS WOULD YOU LIKE TO ASK HIM OR HER?

★ WHAT QUESTIONS DO YOU THINK HE OR SHE MIGHT LIKE TO ASK YOU?

Rapunzel has met a lot of folks on her adventures, and she has learned that there's more to people than meets the eye. File through her gallery and find these faces. Look out—Pascal has blended into 5 of the backgrounds. See if you can spot his portraitbombs!

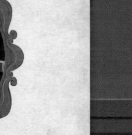

There's more to SEE

THINK AND SHARE!

★ PICK OUT SOME PEOPLE RAPUNZEL FEELS CLOSE TO.

★ WHO IS IMPORTANT IN **YOUR** LIFE?

★ WHEN AND HOW DID YOU FIRST MEET THESE IMPORTANT PEOPLE?

★ WRITE IT! WRITE A FAIRY TALE ABOUT HOW YOU MET YOUR ROLE MODEL, MENTOR, OR BEST FRIEND. BEGIN WITH "ONCE UPON A TIME..."

Rapunzel sometimes finds herself in the middle when it comes to her two best friends, Cassandra and Eugene. It isn't always easy to help good friends find common ground, but it's always worth the effort. Take a look at this outdoor scene and find these items:

these apples

book

targets

this bag

trailer

"WANTED" poster

WANTED

Flynn Rider

Friends
don't let friends

THINK AND SHARE!

★ HOW DOES IT FEEL WHEN TWO PEOPLE YOU KNOW DON'T SEE EYE TO EYE?

★ WHAT DO YOU DO TO HELP?

★ WRITE IT! WRITE A SCENE FROM A PLAY IN WHICH TWO CHARACTERS DON'T GET ALONG. HELP THE TWO CHARACTERS RESOLVE THEIR DIFFERENCES AT THE END OF THE SCENE!

SAVE THE DAY ALONE

Rapunzel's creativity keeps her busy... and never bored! Delve into her design and find these painted creations:

I'm JUST getting STARTED

THINK AND SHARE!

★ WHAT ARE YOUR FAVORITE SONGS, WORKS OF ART, MOVIES?

★ WHO ARE THE MOST CREATIVE PEOPLE YOU KNOW?

★ WHAT DO YOU ADMIRE ABOUT THEM?

★ WHAT DO YOU LOVE BEST ABOUT YOUR OWN CREATIVITY?

Rapunzel never gives up on her dreams, and she adds new ones every day! Her journal is like a friend. It helps her think through her adventures before and after she lives them, like the first time she saw the floating lanterns. Find these lanterns as they rise up through the sky:

LISTEN to your DREAMS

LISTEN to your DREAMS

THINK AND SHARE!

★ FOR RAPUNZEL, EACH LANTERN IS A DREAM COME TRUE. WHAT ARE YOUR DREAMS?

★ DREAMS TAKE WORK! WHAT DO YOU DO TO KEEP YOUR DREAMS AFLOAT?

★ KEEP A JOURNAL! WRITE DOWN YOUR THOUGHTS, FEELINGS, BRILLIANT IDEAS, AND INSPIRATIONS. "FILL YOUR OWN PAGES!"

★ ALWAYS REMEMBER: YOU ARE AMAZING!